ANYBODY ANYWHERE

THE STRANGE CHRONICLES

JENNIFER LAUER

For my late grandmothers
Rosalie Shay & Laura Adams

"You said you're a...vampire, and that you're being framed. Please tell me more about that." My voice is unsteady, as this entire premise feels unbelievable.

"Yes," he says.

"I'm Detective Gray Cooper, please have a seat," I say, looking up at a man who looms at six foot five. He quickly takes a seat on the small orange sofa, which was just delivered to our new office last night. A light chemical smell still lingers in the air.

He crosses his long legs, and his elegance permeates the small office. His cropped Afro hair, and manicured beard are too clean, too perfect. He almost sparkles. He wears a bomber jacket with a long cape.

Joe holds his hand out to Conrad.

"I'm Gray's partner here at Strange Investigations. Call me Joe." He shakes Conrad's hand and winks at me. A drop of happiness hits my chest, because this is exactly what I wanted. A partner with whom I can share inside jokes and winks from across the room that say, *I see you.* The way Joe is comfortable in his skin is appealing, and unlike the exaggerated bravado of many men.

I glance up at the clock, because I'm supposed to be heading to my grandmother's house for lunch. I'd planned to show Joe the new office and expected it to take fifteen minutes. Now I'm going to be late.

Conrad showing up is unexpected.

Him showing up and telling us he's a vampire is unreal.

I've never met a vampire. At least that I know of.

Conrad sits on the couch, I take a seat at my new desk, and Joe perches on the corner of said desk.

"Tell us why you're here," I say.

"Yes, of course. I work at The Crucible," he says. His voice sounds like a melody.

"The coffee shop?" I confirm.

"Yes. Why the unsure look?" he asks. Vampires have jobs at coffee shops. Okay.

"I don't know, suppose I have some preconceived notions about vampires. Apologies," I say.

"We do everything we can to blend in."

"I see, please continue then. You work at The Crucible…"

"Yes. A patron was killed there last week. The police don't have enough evidence to arrest me but told me not to leave town. I think I'm being framed." When he flashes his violet eyes at me, they nearly make me faint. My chest feels warm.

Joe stands and starts to pace.

"Who was the patron?" he asks, and starts to pace.

"Adam Dawson," Conrad says.

I get out my notepad, because I'm old-school.

"Did you know him?" I ask.

"Sure, he's a regular," he says, pushing back the sleeves of his jacket to reveal the tattoos snaking up his arms – black flowers on one arm and thorns on the other.

I take a deep breath. The way he holds eye contact makes my ears burn, I glance over to Joe to see if he is feeling it too. Joe seems unaffected. It's confusing, Conrad's energy sends my Joe flutters into the background.

Focus, Gray.

"Tell us about the night he was murdered," says Joe. He stops pacing and sits in the wooden chair by the window.

Conrad's face squints in discomfort.

"We close at six o'clock, and Adam came in just before that. Ordered his regular red-eye and left. Nothing strange about it at all."

Red-eye in the evening, noted.

"How did he seem? Tired? Happy? Sad?" I ask.

"He seemed ordinary, maybe a little tired. He works a lot; he's mentioned he's the assistant to a prominent politician in Boston."

"Do you know which politician?" I ask.

"Patrick Bennett. He has a house in Salem."

"Did Adam do anything unusual before he left?" I ask.

Conrad thought a minute.

"Not that I recall."

"Okay, then what happened?"

"I wiped down the tables and pushed in the chairs, and I took out the trash." He exhales.

"Did you use the front door or another door?" I ask.

"The side door goes to the alley where the dumpster is." He shivers.

"I opened the dumpster, and started to swing the trash bag in, when I noticed a foot next to the dumpster. I dropped the trash and went to him. He was propped up in a seated position against the wall. I knew it was Adam right away."

"And how did you know he was...dead?" I ask.

Conrad closes his eyes.

"His neck was all torn up. So many cuts. But…there was no blood."

"No blood," I repeat, thinking about what this could mean, especially considering who I am talking to.

"I touched his neck. I couldn't help it." His tone is apologetic and rubs his hand on his thigh as tears fill his eyes.

"It was so sad," he continues. "His eyes were closed, and his skin was so pale. I mean, I saw him most days, and he was always polite and full of energy. And then just like that, his light was out."

There is such weight to each of his words, I feel my own eyes well.

"And then what did you do?" I feel guilty asking him. They didn't talk about this in detective school – how emotional this would be. We talked about questions to ask and what to pay attention to, but we did not discuss how it would feel.

"I ran inside to call the police."

"And what did you do while you waited?"

"I went back outside and stayed with him. There was something so cruel about him being left there, by the trash. Humans are so vulnerable, even in death."

As he says the words, the air becomes electric. A buzzing feeling pulses inside my body, like I'm under a spell. Everything in me wants to comfort Conrad.

"I'm so sorry," I tell him.

"Unlike vampires," Joe says, breaking the spell. Joe eyes the clock. Noticing the time, I realize I cannot stay any longer or I'll miss my visit to Gramma Sugar's. It's been months since I've seen her. I miss her and need her support now more than ever, after my mom's death.

"I believe your story, Conrad," I tell him, because I do.

"So, you'll take the case?" He looks eagerly at me and then to Joe.

Joe defers to me, but his eyes are skeptical. I'm not sure he believes that Conrad is being framed, but regardless this will be a fascinating case – I just know it.

The problem is my priority is finding my father. Knowing that he is alive somewhere, I can't give up on helping him. What would Woody Cooper do?

"Yes, we'll take the case," I say.

2

I rush out to the car and hit my knee on the car door as I get in. It hurts, but I'm too high on the dopamine rush of accepting my next case. This one involves murder, politics, and a very tall and handsome vampire.

While I visit my grandma, Joe stays behind at the plaza and goes to work at Mistwell. He's already taking advantage of the convenience of his insurance company being a few doors down from the detective office.

I'm trying hard not to lean so heavily on the gas, hoping to avoid a speeding ticket. This visit is long overdue, and my shame for not making it sooner sloshes inside my stomach. Gramma Sugar is so important to me, but my immediate reaction to Mom's death was to freeze, and in the process I froze Gramma out.

After an hour, I see a small water tower with the name *Plum* Grove painted on the tank in faded mauve and exit the highway. Plum Grove is north of Salem, and after three very long stoplights, I finally arrive at Gramma Sugar's cottage.

It's been too long since I've seen her. Once I solved my first case and secured the new office, some of the frozen bits defrosted inside me, and I've been able to return to more of my life. I'm looking forward to seeing her more than any other thing in my life.

She was sick with pneumonia and didn't make it to Mom's funeral at the beach. She sent a floral wreath in her stead. When I called to plan this visit, I could tell I'd waited too long. Gramma was terse with me, and now I have to make it right with her.

I hurry up her front walk and jiggle the handle on the storm door, as she opens the main door from the inside.

"Sorry, I'm late," I say as I walk into the house.

Gramma Sugar. She pulls me in and kisses my cheek. Then, she hugs me an extra-long time.

"So sorry about Madeline." Her voice is muffled into my hair.

Mom.

The hug vibrates with grief.

Abruptly, she pulls back and holds my shoulders, sniffing back the emotion of the moment. I do the same.

"Gray," she says giving me a side-eye.

"Yes?" I ask, knowing her look means I've done something she disapproves of.

The memory hits from when I was three-years-old and had spilled grape juice all over her white fabric chair hits me like a bus. My grape-stained mouth lied to her when it said it wasn't me. She said my name with warm suspicion and gave me a look similar to the one she's giving me now.

"You exist. Can I get you tea?" She releases me.

"Yes, I'd love some," I say as I always do. I watch her long gray hair bounce along her back until she disappears into the kitchen.

Gramma Sugar is not exactly what most people expect from a grandmother. She is tall and fit and wears her hair long and curled like Veronica Lake. Her age shows in her wrinkled, makeup-free skin, but her essence is youthful. She's always had boyfriends, ever since my grandfather left when my father and his two sisters were young and she was left to raise them on her own.

My aunts Alex and Red are twins. One moved north to Maine, and the other south to Florida, and every time I see them it's a wild party. They are like living firecrackers, and every visit ends with them in an argument.

Gramma Sugar is well-known in Plum Grove and all over Massachusetts. I'm not sure exactly why, but she will know most people in every room. Everyone calls her Sugar, and for most of my life I thought it was her given name. Her name is actually Sarah —Sarah Cooper. It's nice, but she'll always be Gramma Sugar to me.

"Which mug?" she asks from the kitchen.

"The puppy mug." The one I always choose. It's a small mug in the shape of a basset hound, and one of the floppy ears makes the handle. There is a chip on one side, but I refuse to let her throw it away.

"Don't drink on the chipped side," she warns me for the four hundredth time.

"I won't." I smile.

We take a seat at the small, cramped table in front of the kitchen window, where overgrown aloe plants sit in the sill, as we wait for the water to boil.

"I have some news," I say. There is no reason to continue to dodge the facts that I haven't been answering her calls and haven't visited.

"I'd hoped so."

She knows.

"Gramma, it's about the family business," I say.

"Didn't know there was one." She is coy.

"Well, you know how I got my P.I. certification," I say.

"Yes." Color fills her cheeks, which makes me hesitate for just a moment, because I can't tell if she's happy or mad.

"Well, I did it. I got my business license and an office space, and..." I start.

"Oh, that's my girl." Gramma is giddy. She clasps her hands together in front of her chest, much like I do when I'm excited. I'm so relieved, my shoulders unwind.

"And I'm focusing on paranormal cases. Like Dad," I say.

She inhales deeply, her face changing from relieved to haunted.

"You don't want to be like your father," she says quietly.

I'm not surprised that she thinks this, but I am surprised that she says it out loud. He was always her favorite, and I've never heard her say a bad word about him.

"Why not?" I ask.

"Your father was careless," she says with a bite.

"He's not dead," I say, and her eyes widen.

"You know," she says quietly, clearly startled.

"Gramma, I'm going to find Dad. I know where he is, sort of..." I can't continue. How do I tell Gramma that Dad is in some sort of purgatory hell prison and the way I know is because my dead mother came back as a ghost and told me so?

"Where?" Her whole body stiffens. This is unusual for my physically fluid grandmother.

"It's complicated," I say.

"Gray, I think that I need to tell *you* something." A confession is not what I expected, but her body language has become unreadable and now I don't know what to think. What could she have to tell me? With the way my family situation keeps growing wilder and wilder – she could tell me almost anything right now...

"I'm ready." I plant both hands on the table.

"About the family business," she starts.

Here we go.

"You *just* said you didn't know there was one." This is going well.

"I'll be frank about it. Our family is...special. Meaning we have a certain connection to the other side."

"Can you define 'other side'?'"

"You used, *paranormal.* I suppose that works. You said you think you know where your father is. Well, I know exactly where he is."

"You do?" The fact zips through me.

Gramma Sugar was heartbroken when we got news of Dad's death. Her grief was thick and real.

"Gramma, you were so upset to find out Dad died. We had a ceremony for him. When did you know?"

"I'm very sorry we couldn't tell you. At the time, we had to go along with the story of him being dead for everyone's safety."

So, they all knew but me. My face is stone as my emotions crush together inside.

"You sound like Mom."

She freezes. Oh, no. Should I tell her about Mom? If Gramma has a connection to the other side, maybe she already knows?

"Have you seen Madeline?" she asks.

"Yes and no," I say honestly.

"Have you seen her after her death?"

"Yes." Gramma Sugar takes a deep breath. We both know this visit is about to reveal some big secrets.

The teapot screams to a boil.

3

Gramma Sugar places the pup mug in front of me, and she and I lock eyes in a knowing look.

"I'll get straight to the long and short of it — our ancestors have long been connected to the shadows of this world. Some were called mystics or healers, charlatans or... witches." She lets the last word linger on her tongue.

"And were they?"

"Oh yes, dear."

That's it. I'm from a family of mystics and witches, no big deal.

"And are you one?" I ask her. I'm starting to see Gramma Sugar in a whole new light ... or dark.

"Am I one what, Gray?" Her retort is accusing, yet her eyes sparkle.

"Are you a witch?"

Gramma coughs and bends over in her chair.

"Gramma, are you okay?"

She grabs her chest, still coughing.

"I'm fine, I'm fine, just some tea down the wrong pipe."

She clears her throat.

"I most certainly am not going to categorize myself with some pedestrian label, like witch. Enchantress, perhaps?"

"Gramma, do you have powers?"

"We *all* have powers, dear. The trick, you see, is that very, very few of us ever acknowledge the fact. Few of us ever develop our power and even fewer *use* our power for good."

"And what about Dad?"

"Your father certainly tried to use his powers for good. In fact, maybe he tried a little too hard. Which is what got him into the quite literal peril he currently resides in."

"Why did you wait so long to tell me?"

"It wasn't time until it was. You see, Gray, time is not linear, and our family and our work is not tied to the limits of this world. We are privy to many worlds, all of them happening right within this moment."

"Okay, you lost me."

"Don't worry, you will learn what you need to know, just when you need to know it. Try and remember this when you feel urgent or late – slow down and remember everything will reveal itself exactly when it's meant to be."

Part of me that knows what she's saying is true. The other parts want to scream.

"So, you want me to relax and know I'll receive all the information I need to know when I'm supposed to? And be completely chill about the fact that I'm from a family of mystics and warlocks?"

"Enchantresses," she corrects.

"Gramma."

"But you Gray, you have the legacy intuition. I always knew you did. Your father knew too, but your mother took some convincing."

"What do you mean?"

"Well, it's your power. Like I was saying, we all have one.

Yours is how you see things others might not see. You feel people."

When she says it, I know exactly what she means. I feel people, their aura or vibe. Sometimes it is subtle, sometimes it strikes me like a lightning bolt, and sometimes I need to numb the intensity of it.

"Yes, that feels true. What do I do about it?"

"You use it. For good of course. And you learn to wield it and recover from it. Those are things I can teach you."

"Okay."

"Do you have any questions?"

"Only seven hundred and seventy-seven."

"Oh, the number of divine guidance and completion. Great way to finish the conversation."

"Finish? We haven't even begun the discussion," I say.

"Your tea is getting cold, dear. Why don't you tell me something about your love life?"

"We are not done talking about this."

"I'm sure we're not, but I haven't seen you in too long. I must know if you've had any suitors lately."

"Gramma, I've told you before, I've sworn off dating."

"That is a terrible plan — we'll work on it. What are your hobbies lately?"

"Reading and vodka."

"Not a bad start, but maybe broaden your horizons."

"Well, I'm about to add investigating vampires."

"Now that sounds more like it," Gramma Sugar says with a wicked laugh.

4

The Crucible café, is on Seventh Avenue, an offshoot from Salem Street. A large, stone black cauldron sits on the sidewalk by cafe's door. It serves as a chalk board where the day's specials are listed in neat writing on one side of the bowl. There is a quote written along the rim of the cauldron.

From the darkness comes the urgency of sin, and also the hope of light.

Well, if that doesn't put you in the mood for a double espresso, I don't know what will.

I open the door and step into the shop, which is decidedly void of the urgency of sin. It's clean and cozy, greeting me with the scent of coffee and fresh baked cookies. There are eight cast-iron round tables scattered about, but only two have patrons sitting at them. Black walls hold framed programs from Arthur Miller's *The Crucible*, along with black-and-white headshots of local actors who performed in a Salem production of the play.

It is a marvelous piece of drama, and I've seen it exactly twenty-eight times. Including the time I was in the play myself in high school. I played Sarah Good, one of the first women in Salem to be accused of witchcraft. I remember my favorite line: "You're a liar! I am no more a witch than you are a wizard! If you take away my life, God will give you blood to drink!"

Squirrely, that Sarah Good was.

Apparently, the line was taken directly from the actual witch trials, and the Minister who questioned Sarah Good at trial then died of a blood hemorrhage.

I walk toward the counter.

"Because she was a real witch," I hear a familiar voice say.

I turn around and find my mother standing there.

"You know about the witches too," I say out loud. Mom brings her finger to her lips to hush me. It's not my actual mother, but my mother's ghost, to be precise. I'm surprised to see her here in a public space, but not surprised that she's a ghost. She usually appears in more private spaces; this is something I'm working on getting used to.

The couple at the nearest table look at me strangely, while a woman at the back snickers.

I turn and make my way to the counter, and say under my breath, "What are you doing here?"

"I know you went to see Gramma Sugar."

As I step up to the glass display case counter, I'm greeted by a smiling woman with a short auburn bob. I'm surprised by her demeanor considering the grisly act that happened at her workplace so recently. In fact, I'm surprised The Crucible is open for business at all.

"How can I help you?" she asks.

My mind goes blank. I want to talk to mom but can't easily do it in public.

Order the coffee.

The reason I'm here is to investigate my case. Conrad. The murder.

The barista searches my frazzled expression.

"Need a minute," I say. Or several hours.

Deep breath.

I scan the list of coffee drinks on the blackboard hanging on the wall behind the barista. In the same chalk writing as the quote in front, someone's written dozens of coffee drinks and tea names inspired by characters from the play. Proctor's Pumpkin Latte, Abigail's Americano, Hale's Hazelnut Breve, and Tituba's Tea.

"I'll have an Abigail Americano," I say.

"Sure thing," she says, as she sets to work pouring the espresso shots. While she toils my eyes fall to the glass case, where I see a full plate of freshly baked chocolate chip cookies.

"And a cookie," I add. She gives me an approving nod.

I put in my earbuds, so I can pretend I'm on the phone.

"Mom, I haven't seen you in a week, I thought you had gone for good," I say. Because I did. I wasn't sure where she went, but I thought we'd said goodbye. That she couldn't visit anymore.

"They only allow me to visit when it's essential, when I have a message," she says.

"Gramma Sugar told me everything." I say, sitting down at a table.

"Gray, you should know by now you can't possibly know everything. But you already do know many important things."

"She said I have some sort of legacy intuition?"

"Yes, inherited from your father. We didn't know at first, but then it became undeniable. As a baby, you always had a strong reaction to people. Certain people would make you scream and cry like they injured you, and others you would coo at and adore. I found this to be normal behavior, but your father kept insisting there was something more to it with you. One day, you had a terrible reaction toward the baker at my favorite bakery in town. I'd always found him to be nice and harmless, but he was arrested for arson the next day. That convinced me."

"So, I was a baby psychic, cool. Mom, what is the message?"

"Gray, I came here to tell you..." She began to flicker.

"Mom?" I spoke so loud, it caused everyone in the café to look at me.

"Be c—" And she was gone.

I feel bad I wasted her visit on my own questions. Hopefully, she'll come back and finish her message.

"Abigail Americano and Crucible Cookie ready," the barista calls. I grab them from the counter and head to a table near the side door clearly marked with an Exit sign.

This is the door Conrad said he used to take the trash outside. The door that led to his discovery of Adam.

Watching the barista disappear into the back, I take the opportunity to leave out the side door; my coffee and cookie stay on the table for later.

The cool air hits me like an ice block, and my bones quiver. The alley is quiet. The dumpster bin is to my right, and there's old police tape fluttering on the ground on both sides of it. It's a relatively clean alley, as far as alleys go.

Crossing to the opposite side to the cafe, I take photos of the door and the dumpster.

I walk to the spot where Conrad said he found the victim. There is a tall candle and a couple of dead roses lying in the spot. I take more photos. Squatting, I look around hoping to see something more than pavement.

There is a cold feeling in my gut, like someone is stirring ice cubes inside me. I watch the steam of my breath dance in front of my face. It's almost like my body knows something dark has happened here.

I look in the cracks along the pavement, hoping they'll tell me something. Then I look in the concrete crease between the wall behind the dumpster and the ground, and a glint catches my eye.

It's a tiny spark of light, a reflection of the sun.

I lean my head against the wall to get a better look. Snap a photo. Ruffle through my bag and find my tweezers. Whatever it is, it's tiny. On my first attempt to retrieve it, I drop it. But my second try is a success. It looks to be a piece of confetti, a tiny black circle with sparkles. I bag it and stand up.

Could be nothing, could be something.

Slowly, I inspect the ten-by-ten area around the dumpster for anything else. But I find nothing, police must've been thorough.

I head back inside to my Crucible Cookie and coffee. Sitting at the table, I take a bite of the cookie. It's glorious.

I send Joe a photo of the confetti and tell him I'm at The Crucible.

"I'll have the Proctor's Pumpkin Latte," I hear a familiar voice say to the barista and my stomach sinks. I look to the counter.

He looks over to find me staring.

I stand up quickly, bumping my thigh on the table.

Ouch.

Try to smile through a wince.

"Heath," I manage to get out.

"Of all the café's in all the world," he says. His amber eyes warm the starkness of his police uniform.

Heath Tyler, my ex-fiancé.

5

"What are you doing in Salem?" I demand. He squares his shoulders and his face softens.

"I'm here to see you," he says. He can't be serious.

"You can't be serious."

"I'm sorry about Madeline. I tried to reach out, but you never responded. So, I gave you space," he said.

If he only knew, she was in this exact coffee shop only moments ago.

"Thanks. I'm sorry, I wasn't really responding to anyone," I say, and the burn of all those I've been ghosting deepens. I had seen his text, but he was literally the last person I wanted to talk to.

"I get it. You look good," he says. My face flushes, and I can't help but feel the familiar sensation of a crush — the way the pressed navy shirt fits over his biceps. The sharp lines of his uniform. Heath is an officer with the Massachusetts State Patrol now.

We'd met during orientation at detective school. He was tall and gangly then, hadn't quite filled out from all the crushing workouts and protein-fueled diet that he endured later in the police academy.

I remember how a small group of us sat in a tight circle in the quad, while the leader had us go around and say our names and one unique fact about ourselves. I said proudly I was Gray and my father was a PI, hoping to win brownie points. Heath Tyler told us that when he was at camp as a kid he saw Bigfoot, which garnered laughs and my keen interest. His willingness to share his nerdiness created a stark contrast to his high cheekbones and brooding amber eyes and thick dark hair. He was a hot, dark villain mixed with a dorky sci-fi nerd.

Just my type, apparently.

He asked for my number and so I wrote it on my hand in pen and showed it to him like a brat. He took my hand and pressed it to his, so now a light copy imprinted on his skin. It was very detective-school romance of us.

He called me that night.

What followed was an extremely intense and, looking back, mostly unhealthy relationship. Heath could make me feel like I was the queen of the world, and because of that, when things were bad in his life, I felt completely insignificant to him.

We got engaged after one year of dating. We planned on detective careers and children. He went off to the police academy, while I procrastinated on my career, planning our life together. One week before his graduation, we broke up. We both said things we'd regret, and I called his bluff on ending it.

Unfortunately, the breakup did a number on my desire to become a detective. I had lost myself with Heath, and have only recently begun to find myself again. And for him to turn up so unexpectedly, it's just thrown me off completely.

"Why are you here?" I ask.

"I wanted to see you. Well, not actually right at this

moment. I planned to call you, but I feel like maybe running into you was meant to be," he says. Old energy dances between us.

"Why did you want to see me?"

"I want to tell you I'm getting married," he says. Again my gut drops.

"You came all the way here to tell me you're getting married." I blink hard.

"Well, yes. Not exactly 'all the way here.' Elizabeth is from Marblehead, and that's where the wedding will be. It's not too far, so I thought I'd come back to Salem and let you know in person," he says.

"Okay, you did it. Happy for you." I'm not. I don't know what I feel, but happy is certainly not it. I cross my arms awkwardly.

"Gray, I'm sorry about how things ended with us and just want you to know I'm here for you," he says. A small part of me still wants to believe he's here with goodwill, but it is over-ridden by the bigger part of me.

"Thanks," I say diplomatically.

He leans in close, and I can smell his Burberry aftershave, originally a gift from his dad but he's clearly continued using it. His body language feels familiar, like *he is going to kiss me*.

He pecks me on the cheek, and as he leaves, he shoulders past the man who just entered.

It's Joe Nebraska.

6

oe's face lights up when he sees me, and my cheeks flush.

"Thanks for coming — you're so punctual," I joke.

My eyes can't help but follow Heath's frame as he walks past the window, and his glance back hits mine.

Joe notices.

"You know that guy?" he asks.

Yes, almost married him.

"No," I say. The truth in this moment is too fraught. We sit at the table, and I hold onto my coffee and cookie for dear life.

"Are you going to get anything?" I ask.

"No, just ate. Let's see this confetti."

I take the baggie out of my bag and hold up my possible clue. Joe inspects it closely.

"I know where this is from," he says.

"You're kidding."

"The Royal Icon. VIP suite. A club in Boston."

I'm speechless.

"What?" He smiles.

"How do you know this?"

"Part of their VIP *experience* is to unleash an obscene amount of confetti when a bottle of Bollinger-something champagne is opened. We had a claim at Mistwell against the club because some influencer cut her hands on a broken bottle."

"Mistwell represents clubs in the city?"

"We do. Being a smaller company, we can maintain flexibility, which gives our clients a more tailored experience."

"Nice pitch."

Joe smirks. And I'm truly impressed that he put this all together.

"Should we go take a look at the crime scene?" He points to the side exit.

"Most definitely."

As we walk toward the door, a new barista exclaims loudly, "I'm feeling your trenchcoat energy. You look so good!" I blush and feel everyone stare at me. Sometimes I forget I'm wearing it; I've had it for so long it feels just natural to have it on.

Also, I truly need to learn to take a compliment, since it always feels so uncomfortable. One little kindness puts me into a spiral.

It seems like a manipulation — if I say these pretty words to you, what will you do for me? Always conditional. My entire life I have dismissed kind words as acts of malevolence, even when I desperately want them. And have given them freely to others.

I think it's about trust. Do I trust you mean it? And what does it mean if you do? Am I lovable? Like, is my truest, deepest self good enough? The self who isn't trying to please you?

My parents gave me praise when I was young. I wonder why I didn't believe them either?

My new plan is to start trusting more. If someone is malevolent, I'll wait till I see it to judge it.

I'm a goddamn detective.

If kind words are used toward me, I'll accept them and be grateful and continue sending my own goodness out in earnest.

Maybe this is the way to unconditional love? To accept it from a barista on a cold day in Massachusetts?

"Thank you," I tell her, and leave it there.

Joe and I step down into the alley, and I watch him look around like I did.

"Where did you find the confetti?" he asks.

I take him over to the wall and point.

"In that crack? Jesus. How? Gray, you're really good at this."

Two compliments in quick succession. My plans collapse.

"I haven't solved it yet, so 'really good' isn't accurate."

Joe sighs and takes some of his own photos.

I didn't say I was going to be a gold-star compliment taker anytime soon.

7

Sitting alone in my car Hero, I stare at my phone. I want to call my best friend, Lucy. She's the only one I can talk to about my run-in with Heath. But it has been so long. Why is it the longer you wait before getting back to someone, the harder it is to make the call? Lucy has only ever been kind and patient with me, and I've avoided her for too long.

There is so much I need to catch her up on — Mom and Strange Investigations ... Joe ... Heath. My finger hovers over her name, when I receive a message. It's from Conrad. The Vampire.

Hi Gray. I found out there is an event tonight, and Patrick Bennett's new assistant will be there. Think we should go?

We. Well, this is a great opportunity for the case. We can question the assistant, maybe find out if Conrad is correct in assuming the politician is indeed the one framing him. Although, I've never gone out at night with a vampire.

Should be completely fine. Super fun. I'll love it.

I message back:

Conrad, that sounds great. Time/place?

10pm. The Royal Icon. Dress hot, he answers.

This is definitely not the professional exchange I was trained for in detective school. First of all, The Royal Icon — the place where the confetti came from? At least, this is what Joe thinks. I could be meeting the bad guy tonight, and I'm giddy at the thought of being closer to solving my first actual murder case. Ten o-clock to *start* the night. This is going to require more caffeine. What does 'hot' mean to a vampire who looks ten years younger than me, but is likely a couple hundred years older?

I respond with, *Great, see you then.*

He replies, *Just a warning, this will be dangerous.*

Well, you had me at warning. I suppose I'll be adding some protective layers to my *hot* outfit. It does occur to me I might want to tell Joe about this, but the threat of danger has me reconsidering, because he might talk me out of it.

And I might let him.

8

I take an Autovehicle into the city to avoid dealing with the parking situation. I get out at an intersection in the industrial area of Boston, where concrete buildings loom. Walking past an abandoned factory, in my equally hot and uncomfortable black suede thigh-high boots. I paired the boots with a short, fitted, soft black leather dress and sheer black tights. The dress gives off sexy vibes while also being practical, the material is easy to move in and has a couple of secret zip pockets on the sides.

The building ahead of me heralds a plaque that says '3,' while I'm looking for 1 Commonlack Avenue. It does not exist in the city map system, but Joe represented this club, so I know it's real.

I take the corner past 3 Commonlack and in a poorly lit alley, a couple leans against a wall in the distance. The faint sound of a bass beat is thumping; it emanates from somewhere nearby.

My phone buzzes. It's Joe.

I told him where I was going after all, and he was not

thrilled. In the end, he asked if I'd call him when I get home. I agreed.

Joe's message reads, *I hope you had a garlic sandwich for dinner.*

I reply, *Garlic ice cream.*

Yum, says Joe.

I smile.

After nearly tripping on the cobblestone, I grip the building. I catch a glimpse of a shadow forming behind me, and I turn quickly.

It's Conrad.

"Oh," I say, relieved.

"Hi, Gray," he says in a silky tone.

He gently takes my elbow to help me stabilize myself, and we walk slowly down the alley.

"There are some things you should know about tonight," he says.

"Go on."

"You know it's not a typical club?" he asks.

"You mean, loud music, lasers, thirsty singles and too much alcohol?" I half-joke.

"It's a feeding night."

"Pardon?" A chill runs up my thighs beneath my tights.

"A night for my kind."

"Okay, can you get back to the 'feeding' part?"

"The patrons are *only* my kind, except..." He takes a necklace out of his pocket and offers to put it over my head.

"What's that?"

"It's your lifeline." I dip my head forward, and he places it around my neck. The place where his fingertips touch my clavicle turns to goosebumps. A small onyx charm dangles from the chain in the shape of a pyramid.

"A totem. It signals that you belong to me. It will keep you safe. People at this club without a totem are free for the taking." My eyes widen.

"So, I wear this necklace, and I belong to you?" I'm suddenly having second and third thoughts about all of this, while also feeling a flutter of exhilaration.

"Well, not truly," he says, and laughs. "Just for tonight." His eyes twinkle.

"Do the non-totem wearing patrons *know* they are on the menu?"

"Oh, yes. And most of the time, they regret their decision."

The chill that went up beneath my tights earlier continues straight into my heart.

"You need to stay close to me. If we get separated for any reason, that is when you leave."

"If these are the guys framing you, aren't they going to cause trouble?"

"I don't believe they think about me at all, whoever it is. My guess is they just used me for convenience, because I work there. They won't expect me to be here, but I do plan to keep a low profile. Meanwhile you get close to them, see if you can glean anything investigative. Then we go."

"Wow, okay. Any other ominous warnings?"

"One more thing — don't drink anything."

"What do you mean? Not even water."

"No liquid. Nothing."

"Well, this sounds like a fun night out. Lucky for me I brought this." I dip my fingers inside the top of my left boot and produce a thin rose gold flask. Unscrew the cap and take a swig and offer it to Conrad.

"Vodka."

He shakes his head.

"Alright, so ... Keep the totem on, don't drink anything and stay close. Got it."

"Are you ready?"

"As I'll ever be."

I slip my arm inside the crook of his elbow, and he leads me to a large metal door with no handle.

It opens without prompting, and we are blasted with cool air and pink lighting. The lights are flashing and a low, deep beat pulses through me, replacing my own heartbeat.

9

Once we are inside, the room feels like a living organism. Writhing bodies, hypnotic music and a completely disorienting light show.

"Stay close," Conrad reminds me. His lithe frame weaves between people. Each time I make eye contact with someone, I'm overwhelmed with everyone's otherworldly beauty. The air is thick with something I can't quite name. Sort of a boozy angst. They all look both embodied and at the same time like they're searching. Wanting.

They're hungry.

Conrad seems to know where he is going. He clasps my hand and leads me through the crowd. We get to a high-top table near the bar and sit on tall chairs. He eyes the stairwell next to us and mouths *VIP*.

We take a minute to look around at this cinematic scene.

I spot a woman with perfect, shiny auburn hair wearing a sparkling angel halo headband. She's dancing with three men. Freckles make constellations upon her cheeks. One of the men has her necklace in his mouth, and I realize it's her totem. He notices me watching and winks at me. My face flushes, and I feel dizzy.

I'm not sure what I expected, but it wasn't ... this. I reach for my flask, and Conrad laughs at me.

"Are you feeling okay?"

"Yes, um, I'm fine," I lie. This place makes me feel drugged all on its own.

Suddenly, the most stunning woman I've ever seen in real life approaches our table. She has flawless skin and long braids down to her waist. Her dark black eyes are shaped like almonds and she's wearing a scowl.

"Conrad," she whisper-spits.

"Asha." He melts. I feel the heat of her gaze as her eyes look me over and land on the totem around my neck. Her nostrils flare.

Conrad's silky demeanor turns flustered. I suppose even the immortal have relationship troubles.

She lets out an audible breath, flips her hair and turns to leave. Judging from her abrupt arrival and departure, I offer him my guess.

"Ex-girlfriend?" I ask.

"Something like that ..." He trails off.

"She's gorgeous."

"Asha is possessive. She doesn't allow people their sovereignty."

"Do you still love her?"

He laughs.

"Love has little to do with it."

"How so?"

"Well, for us, love is only a small part of our relationships. We aren't like humans in that way."

"What are the bigger parts?" I ask, enthralled by the idea of love as a mere appendage.

"Obsession, blood bonds, and destiny," he says, his gaze growing intense.

Well, yes, of course. Sounds like the makings of a completely healthy relationship.

"Not sure those are pillars I'd want to live by," I admit.

"You don't." The volume of the music bumps higher.

His serious eyes soften into smile eyes. He leans in close; his slender fingers gently grip my face as he pulls me in. His voice deepens in my ear.

"Those stairs behind us lead up to the VIP room, and I assume that's where you'll find our guy."

Oh right, this is a job. I'm investigating a case.

"What's his name?"

"Izzy. Not sure on the surname, but he's the new assistant to Lieutenant Governor Patrick Bennett."

"So, I'll chat up Izzy while you watch my back for any vampires looking for a snack?"

"If you have a problem, just touch the totem, and I'll come and get you."

"Got it, thanks."

I head for the stairs and then pause.

"Wait. How will you see me, if I'm up there and you're down here?"

Conrad looks up, and I follow his line of sight. There are several well-dressed club goers floating and socializing near the ceiling.

"No freaking way. You can fly?"

"Levitation."

I look up again to the dozen or so levitating vampires.

"Why aren't more up there? Is it a rare trait?"

"Oh, no. Most don't do it much, if at all. Can you imagine if one made it a habit? It would make them more vulnerable to an accidental public display. And well, it would be catastrophic for all of us. Protecting our kind is a pillar of our existence."

"Wow. Well, good to know that you have me covered."

He grins. "I do."

Vampires freaking *fly*. I have so many questions. But they'll have to wait.

I continue to head up the stairs. As I near the top of the staircase, I realize I'm about to enter a private room with a bunch of vampires. A fever burns through me as I open the door and slip inside. No one seems to notice my entrance to my great relief. People clustered in small groups mix and chat.

It's a large room with black velvet couches. At the front of the room is an open balcony overlooking the club, and the levitating vampires are mingling around the edges just outside. In front of the opening is a wide leather couch, where several men and one woman all wearing sunglasses sit.

It smells like smoke. A familiar chill runs up the back of my neck, as I consider the potential of Zeke's presence. Zeke, is a foul being who has taken ownership of my father's possessions. But as I scan the room, I see no sign of him.

Relieved, I look down and see the floor is nearly covered in the same kind of confetti I found at the murder scene. Bending down as demurely as I can, I grab some confetti and put it in a tiny zip pocket on the side of my dress.

A man in a suit and overly gelled hair approaches me with a wicked furrow in his brow. But when he gets close, his eyes go straight to the totem around my neck and he keeps walking past me to the small bar on my left.

Then I hear a high-pitched squeal of laughter and a woman say, "Okay, Izzy, sure."

Izzy.

He's sitting on a second couch just behind the large sunglass couch. Izzy is flanked by two women in sequins, while he's wearing a gray suit with a skinny tie. His hair is reddish with a deep side-part, combed to create a voluminous pouf. He has tired eyes, although he looks to be late twenties. He clenches his jaw, and his shoes are expensive. The woman in red sequins gets up and leaves. Here's my chance.

The only problem is that I haven't had the time to think up a good cover story or a reason I'm up here at all. I was too distracted by Conrad to prepare, and now I'm here and I need to make something happen.

Gray, you can do this.

As I move closer, he eyes me from boot tip to hair. The hungry look of a vampire is not easy to get used to. It feels both invasive and alluring. I wonder why the Lt. Governor would have a vampire assistant after his last one, the recently departed, Adam Dawson, was a human.

Too delicate, perhaps.

"Who do we have here?" Izzy asks.

"May."

"Hello, May. Please have a seat."

My heart races, despite my effort to take slow breaths. He eyes the totem.

"I haven't seen you in here before."

"I haven't seen you either." I smile so big I show my teeth, remembering that this is my mark. Suddenly, he grips my wrist hard and leans his face close to mine.

"What are you doing up here?"

I glance over his shoulder and spot Conrad just outside the corner of the balcony. You better come up with a story, and you better do it quick. His hand squeezes my wrist harder; my heart thuds in my ears.

Something. Say something, Gray.

"Drugs," I say, surprising myself.

"Drugs?" he asks, releasing the tight grip on my wrist.

I slide my hand into my right bootleg and present a small Ziploc bag filled with red tablets.

"What is it?"

"Boss calls them Candy."

He's not going to fall for that. Be more creative. He offers me the palm of his hand. I give him one, and he swallows it.

"Smells like Christmas. What do they do?"

"What don't they do?" I reply.

He gets out his phone, I take out mine, and he sends me 500 Coin. I give him my stash. Damn. It has to be the most expensive bag of cinnamon candy ever.

He offers the open bag to me, and I take two candies. Then he hands the bag to the girl in blue sequins, who promptly takes one and scurries off to share it with someone in the corner. Looks like I'll have to make our conversation quick, before he realizes a sugar high wasn't what he paid for.

"So, Izzy, what do you do when you're not here charming the locals?"

"I work in politics."

"Wow, that is so interesting."

"Very top secret." His hand moves to rest on my thigh. It is a torture I endure.

"Oh, I'll bet."

"And dangerous."

"Dangerous...how?"

"Last guy who had my job died."

"No way."

"Way."

I gasp, lifting my eyebrows in faux surprise. "How did he die?"

He looks around like he's going to tell me his greatest secret. The sunglasses are all ignoring him completely. I can still see Conrad's silhouette near the balcony.

"Murdered."

I wonder how he wants me to respond and go with shock.

"Whoa. You must be really, really brave."

Izzy rubs his hands together, his face smug at the thought. Bingo.

"Yeah. Yes, I am brave."

God, I cannot believe this is working, but now that he's buttered up, I need some information.

"Did they catch the person who did it?"

"It was definitely not a person."

"What do you mean?"

"The way he was clawed up ..." He trails off.

"Not a person?"

He taps my totem with his index finger twice. Hard.

"Hey," I say, grasping my neck.

The second I touched the totem, Conrad is on Izzy, pinning him to the couch by his neck.

"Go, Gray."

I take off toward the stairs and look back to see the sunglasses all stand up and rush toward Conrad and Izzy.

I slip down the stairs as fast as my stiletto boots can take me, but as I start to pass our table, I stop. I can't leave Conrad here. Especially, now that I know Izzy saw Adam Dawson after he was killed. I sit down and tap my fingers nervously. I hear some yelling from upstairs, but a few seconds later, Conrad comes down the stairs looking calm as can be.

"Everything alright?" I ask skeptically.

"We should go," he says.

His hand softly traces my shoulders as he escorts me back through the crowd. When we head down the hallway, I see an open doorway, and as we pass by I look in. A blonde woman in a red jumpsuit and no totem sits in a gold chair, her eyes wide in horror, I can't see who she's staring at and then a black cape covers her face. Once we are past, I hear a guttural scream. She's in trouble. I turn quickly to go back, but Conrad grabs my arm.

"She's in danger," I say, as the screams only come louder.

"No. She chose this. I told you, they always regret the taking," he says.

"She can change her mind." I push his hand away and rush back to the room, preparing myself for a fight. The screaming has stopped. When I'm inside, I see that it's empty. A spatter of blood sinks into the gold velvet chair. Conrad appears in the doorway.

"She's gone," I say.

"I know."

We leave the room and head for the exit. I am so done with vampire night; this place feels like a nightmare come to life. Making our way through the people lining the hallway, we come face-to-face with Asha. She presses her hand to Conrad's chest.

"I need to speak with you."

"It's not a good time."

She looks at me.

"It's urgent."

Conrad looks to me apologetically.

"It's cool, I'll wait by the door."

"Don't move," he says.

"Got it."

I watch Asha and Conrad disappear back into the crowd, then I return to the front door. It's the one spot in the whole place not swimming with hungry bodies. There's a Victorian chair behind a rack of coats, where I take a seat and empty my flask.

As I fasten it back into my boot, Izzy shows up. Deep-red

scratches are streaked across his neck, and he looks less confident.

"Gray May," he says in a sour tone.

Taking stock of my surroundings, I search for some sort of weapon, but there are only coats and the chair I'm sitting on. To my right, I spot an umbrella leaning against the wall. Izzy stands just inches in front of me.

"What are you doing at The Royal Icon?" he asks.

"Just out for a fun night," I deflect.

"Who are you?"

"No one." I'm trying to decide how much he knows about me at this point.

"Where's your boyfriend?"

So he knows I'm interested in the murder, and I'm not some random doll at the club. Maybe I can squeeze this lemon for a little more juice.

"Let's not do small talk. I'll be straight with you: I'm a friend of the guy who died at the coffee shop and want to know what happened to him."

A look of suspicion falls across his face, like he is realizing my lie in real time.

"Your friend crossed the wrong guy."

He lunges at me, and I swing to my right and grab the umbrella and crack him in the ribs. He doesn't expect my speed or weapon and falls down.

When I get up to run, my boot clips the floor, and I stumble. Izzy gets up as I go down. I try to reach inside my boot, but he grasps my arm, and pushes it to the floor. He leans on my torso, and I clutch for my totem.

But my neck is bare.

My stomach drops.

No.

"Conrad—" I start to yell, but the loud beat of the music

drowns me out. He presses his hand tightly over my face, blocking my mouth and nose.

I can't breathe. Stars start to dance around the edges of my vision.

The music becomes muted.

And I slip away.

10

"**G**ray. Gray, darling," I hear my mother say.

I can't quite open my eyes yet, it feels too difficult. My eyelids flutter, but they feel as though concrete has been poured onto them.

I hear banging.

Like my mother is banging a pan against my headboard.

Bang. Bang. Bang.

"Mom, stop." I sit up and rub my eyes, trying to free them.

And then I hear him. He's muffled.

"Gray, Gray, it's me, open up."

Finally, I'm able to let the sunlight in. I push the covers back and stand up, unsteady on my feet. My dress and boots sit in a pile by my bathroom door, and I'm wearing an unfamiliar shirt and nothing else. When I stumble out to the living room, Conrad sits shirtless on my cozy chair.

"I would get the door but didn't think it was my place."

What is happening?

Bang. Bang. Bang.

I unlock the front door, and Joe takes in a breath, looking relieved.

"Jesus, Gray, I thought I was going to have to take the door down."

"Hi, Joe," is all I can muster.

My heart softens at his concern, and I reach my arms up to hug him. He pulls me in tight, and I can feel his heart beating so quickly. He feels like home. We part and as he steps inside the door he spots Conrad.

Joe stiffens.

"Oh. I'm sorry, I didn't realize." He backs up.

"It's not... Nevermind." I don't know what else to say.

"Are you okay?" he gives me a long look.

"Yes. I'm fine, just a long night." I wince.

"Glad you're okay," he says and leaves.

The last five minutes of my life have been such a tornado, I'm considering I might be dreaming. I wring my hands, and turn to Conrad, who sits completely content, despite me and Joe and last night.

"What just happened?" I ask.

"Joe likes you," he says. A tingle of delight runs through me at the thought. However, the last person I'm going to talk to about Joe is our half-naked vampire client, whose shirt I'm wearing for some reason.

"What happened last night?"

"You don't recall?" he asks, genuinely surprised I don't remember.

"No," I say, thinking back to my last memory of the night.

God. Izzy's hand over my mouth.

"Let's just say I hired you to keep me from being pinned as a murderer, and last night I almost became one."

"You hurt Izzy?"

"Yes. What happened to your totem?"

"It must have fallen off when we fought. I'm sorry."

"No, I'm sorry. It wasn't worth going there."

"Oh, but it was," I say as I go into my room. I pull some sweatpants from my dresser and pull them on.

"Izzy knew the body had been roughed up. He noted Adam Dawson had *claw marks*, information not released to the public. Also, he said and I quote, that Adam 'crossed the wrong guy.' Which makes me wonder, who did he cross and what did Adam Dawson do that got him killed?"

I get my own shirt and shut the bedroom door to change into it. When I come out, I hand Conrad his shirt, and our hands pass over each other. A spark like electricity ignites my skin. His eyes penetrate mine, and I'm hypnotized. My head snaps up, like I just caught myself from falling.

"Nothing happened ... between us?" I ask.

"No."

"My clothes?"

"That was you."

Heat rushes to my face, as I realize what he's saying. But usually, one flask does not render my memory obsolete.

"But your shirt." I brace for the explanation.

"I'm a gentleman." This makes me laugh. A gentleman and a vampire, can the two states coexist inside one being? I'm willing to allow for the paradox, because I want to escape this conversation more than I want to know the details of what I did.

"Well, I appreciate you, but you have to go," I say. I have work to do and explanations to make and cases to solve.

And Joe to deal with.

"Thank you for entertaining me. I'm actually feeling confident about the case," Conrad says with a grin.

"Me too."

11

With the distraction of Conrad out of my apartment, I grab my trench and my laptop and head out the door. I drive straight over to The Crucible, deciding to do my work here for two reasons.

1. It's the crime scene.
2. That cookie was incredible.

After I order, I take the seat by the side door and crack open my laptop. I must have missed something about Adam Dawson that will help me. He grew up in Salem, went to college in Boston where he studied languages, lived with his parents, and was the assistant to the lieutenant governor, who hires vampires.

I scroll through his social media photos; everything looks average. Photos with friends, him and his cat, a few from vacations. It's almost like I've seen these pictures before, because they're familiar. Isn't it funny how most of us live very similar lives. When you're not comparing yourself to others, it's easy to see yourself inside many existences. Essentially, we all appreciate the same things: people we love; beautiful places, usually in nature; celebrations and milestones; cute animals and babies; and most especially cute baby animals. Humans are simple in our delights.

I keep scrolling, until I see it. Full stop.

I zoom in on a photo taken in the summer. He's on the beach. Beautiful place in nature — check.

He has on a familiar necklace.

Adam Dawson was wearing a totem. It's a different shape than mine was, but they all have a similar rune with a tapered charm.

Someone nearby clears their throat. I got so lost in photo searching that I didn't realize two figures were loitering by my table waiting for me to look up.

It's Heath and a woman. *Why is he here again?* This time he's out of uniform, wearing black trousers and a tight black tee shirt, and the studded designer belt I got him for our first Christmas as a couple.

Snapping the computer closed, I try to stand up and hit my thighs on the table in the same spot as before as I awkwardly stumble and rise.

"Gray, I'd like you to meet Elizabeth."

"Oh, hi," I say, reaching out my hand.

Elizabeth is the kind of pretty that makes your eyes hurt, like you're staring at the sun. She's got auburn hair and bright, curious eyes. Her freckles look like little constellations. The hairs on my arms stand on end, as recognition washes over me.

It's her. From the Royal Icon. The woman with the angel halo.

I avert my eyes to the floor; afraid she might recognize me too.

"Thought we'd stop by on the off chance you might be here. You a regular or something?" Heath asks.

"Or something," I say. He grabs Elizabeth's waist tightly.

"Heath has told me so much about you. We came here yesterday morning too. They have the best cookies," Elizabeth gushes. "I'll be right back." She turns to go to the counter.

I sigh, relieved that she doesn't seem to recognize me.

"So, what do you think?" Heath asks.

"Beautiful," I say. He looks so self-satisfied and I'm not sure he deserves my concern. I look at him, trying to decide if he knows about his fiancée's extracurricular vampire activities. There's no way. Heath is so by-the-book, he wrote it.

"Do you trust her?" I can't help but ask.

"Completely," he says smugly, and it takes all my self-control to leave it there, even though I want to explain myself because I'm sure he reads the question as jealousy. Soon enough, Elizabeth bounces back into place next to him. And I see it dangling around her neck — the coiled serpent charm with ruby stones for eyes.

"Very unique necklace." I nod to her totem. She fingers it.

"She got it from her dad," Heath announces proudly. She sure did.

"My father died last year," Elizabeth says, suddenly sullen.

"I'm sorry to hear that," I say.

"I'm so lucky to have a dear family friend to walk me down the aisle."

"You're so fortunate," I say, sounding robotic, and I can't help but wonder if her family friend has fangs and can levitate.

"Heath wants to ask you something." She jabs Heath in the ribs.

I look down at my pen. *He wants me to take this pen and stab it through his eye? Or maybe you want me to be the flower girl?*

"Gray, we'd be honored if you would come to the wedding."

Is he serious? I would never, ever go to his wedding.

"Oh, wow. Thanks, but..."

"It's Saturday."

"*This* Saturday?" As in six days from now?

"Yes, isn't it exciting?" he says.

Yes, I hope it's exciting for you. I am still processing the fact that you are in the same room as I am, with your soon-to-be wife, who I just saw gyrating with vampires at a club. That's what I want to say, but instead, I only manage to get a few words out.

"I don't think —"

"I'll send you the details. Just let us know ASAP, we'd love to have you. Bring Lucy, or whoever." And they turn and leave.

The mention of my best friend Lucy feels like a dagger. I've been a terrible friend to her since my mother died. It's partly because the grief made me freeze, and if I'm honest it's partly because she's training to be a therapist. Not only does she see right through me, but she knows exactly how to comfort me. The absence of Lucy has meant the absence of comfort.

"So nice meeting you," Elizabeth sings as they walk out.

Let us know ASAP? Who invites their ex-fiancée to their wedding the week before? And he made such a big deal of asking in person? Who does this?

Heath does.

He thinks the entire world rotates around him. I don't have more important things to worry about than him and his Elizabeth, the vampire fucker. He can't imagine that I have a perfectly imperfect life that I have been navigating happily and unhappily without the disruption of his stupid, perfect face.

I sit back down in front of my computer, but I can't focus

on the case. The fact that Adam Dawson had a totem, Elizabeth has a totem, and hell, even I wore a totem. My eyes float up to the TV screen in the corner of the shop. The news is on, with closed captioning.

Breaking news comes on and says there has been an arrest in the Adam Dawson murder. I stand back up. They are tucking a tall, slim gentleman into a cruiser. Fuck.

It's Conrad.

12

"Joe, it's me Gray. I've tried calling all day. If you're not answering because of Conrad, nothing happened. Well, a lot happened at the club which I'm calling to tell you about. But nothing between me and our client. Call me."

Could Joe really be dodging me, because he's upset about Conrad? It's not like we are dating. Even if it feels like we we've been heading that way. My stomach still feels sick over it.

I phone Mistwell.

"Mistwell Insurance?" It's Blake, the secretary.

"Hi Blake, Gray here. Is Joe around?"

"Nope."

"Do you know where he is?"

"Nope."

"You are so helpful."

"Thanks. He did say he was working a case."

"A Mistwell case or a Strange Investigations case? Wait, let me guess, you don't know."

"Nope."

"If he checks in, can you please have him call me?"

"'Kay."

We hang up and I realize I'm squeezing the pressure point on my hand between my thumb and index finger.

I pick up my bag and keys and start for the door, on my way to the police station to visit Conrad.

My phone rings. I'm expecting Joe when I pick up. "Hey."

"Is this Gray Cooper?"

"Yes."

"I'm calling from Plum Grove Hospital. We have admitted a Sarah Cooper, and you're listed as her next of kin."

Gramma Sugar. Oh god.

"I'll be there in thirty minutes."

13

The hospital smells like rubbing alcohol and soup, as I make my way to Gramma Sugar's room. 317.

It reminds me of my days working as a nursing home aide, before detective school. The fluorescent lighting is a migraine risk, but it is familiar.

Back then, I was full of enthusiasm because my work felt meaningful. On many days it was. I fondly remember reading romance novels to Len, a man who had outlived most of his relatives and lost his eyesight.

The first time I met Len I'd been working at the nursing home for a few weeks and was sent to his room to take his vitals. But he was so starved for attention, he convinced me to stay and chat with him about the passing of his bunkmate Marty. Each time I got up to leave, Len started a whole new conversation to keep me there. He told me reading was the thing he missed most after his eyesight went and asked if I could read him something.

There were no books in the room, except for a romance paperback left on the windowsill Len said was left by Marty's daughter, something called *Dangerous Touch* by J.L. Ivanov.

When I began to read it, Len's face settled into the deepest grin. His entire body relaxed, and when we got to the racy bits he'd say, "Oh, my." And we'd laugh, and sometimes he said "Ohmymymy." The number of 'my's' directly correlated to the sexual explicitness of the passage.

When I'd entered the room, Len had been full of anxiety and sadness about the loss of his roommate and truly desperate to keep me talking to him. It was such an honor to watch him transform into a calmer person after we spent some time reading.

After that, we read the entire backlist of Ivanov. I miss Len.

I realize I've been standing outside room 317 instead of going inside. I'm not sure what I'll find in there. Gramma is the last living stronghold in my life. I expect the worst, to see her hooked up to monitors and teetering on the edge of death. Or worse — the bed will be empty bed and she's gone. *Gramma Sugar, I need you to be alright.* I grasp the handle and push open the door.

I am greeted by neither doom scenario.

"Gray." She smiles. She's sitting up in bed with a full face of makeup and painting her fingernails blue.

"Gramma Sugar?" I take an uneasy breath.

"What do you think?" She wiggles her fingers, showing off her new polish color.

"Powder blue, looks great," I say, going in to hug her.

"More like periwinkle. Nurse let me borrow it. Careful of the nails," she says, reprimanding me. She gives me a half-hug.

"Gramma, what happened? Are you okay?" I ask. "They didn't give me any details."

"Oh, yes, I'm just great. Had to upgrade the old ticker to run on robot technology apparently." She taps her heart.

"Pacemaker?"

"Yes, dear. I'm a little sore, but I feel great actually. Wonder if they could bring us some tea." She presses the Nurse button on the blue wristband she's wearing.

"How long do they think you have to be here?"

"Said I could go tomorrow, just have to stay overnight for observation."

Seeing her alert, alive and active is such a relief I melt into the chair by her bed. My eyes flood with tears.

"Here we go, open the floodgates." I hear a familiar voice that is not Gramma Sugar's.

"Mom?" I sit up straight.

Gramma Sugar and I both look to the stool in the corner of the room, where my mother sits. I rub my face.

"Gray, darling, must you react every single time I visit?" she says.

Before I can speak, Gramma Sugar says, "Give the girl a break. She's had a certain set of expectations about her reality for her entire life, which you so casually shattered. Typical." Gramma Sugar says it like we are in her kitchen and not in a hospital conversing with a ghost.

"Wait, you can see her too?" I ask.

My mom and Gramma look at me incredulously.

"Yes, dear." Another secret door opens in my mind, in my life.

"Wow. Well, since you're both here, I should tell you — Heath is in town." I brace myself for their reactions: Gramma good, and Mom not so good.

"You saw him?" Mom is aghast. An aghast ghost.

"Yes...He's getting married," I say, not liking the way the words feel as they tumble out.

"Was he wearing his uniform when you saw him?" Gramma wags her eyebrows.

"Jesus, Gramma, lie down. You're sick." Gramma Sugar

always had a sweet spot for Heath, especially when he wore his police uniform. However, Mom rolls her eyes. She knows the truth about Heath, the heartbreak, and toll our breakup had on me.

"Well, if he's going to get married, I hope he's had extensive therapy," Mom says.

"Unlikely. I met her too," I say, my heart tightening. The memory of Elizabeth dancing with vampires and wearing a totem that means she *belongs* to one of them, all the while, she is about to marry to my asshole of an ex. I don't hate him enough to let him be eaten by vampires.

At the exact same time I'm thinking this, my maternal guides speak.

"Are you okay?" they say in tandem.

"I'm fine," I lie.

"Gray, you are not fine. I hate to leave the issue here, but as you know, I can only visit when I have a message."

Gramma Sugar inhales deeply.

"Did you tell her?" Mom looks to Gramma Sugar.

"About what exactly?" Gramma says.

"Vampires."

"We didn't get that far..." Gramma trails off.

"My case involves a very respectful vampire, being setup in a murder case," I say and think of Conrad. I see him being put into the police vehicle in my mind. Now I know Gramma is okay, I've got to go and see him.

"Gray. Never trust a vampire."

"That's your message? Sounds like a public service announcement. Conrad is a good vampire. But yes, I have met some bad ones."

Mom crosses her arms.

"Vampires are dangerous in ways you can't see. They charm you and feed off your goodness. They will make you feel euphoric, but it's a trick. It's an anesthetic so you don't notice their intent, until it's too late."

I think of how my body reacted to being in the same room with Conrad, and how I felt at the club. Everything buzzed.

"I can handle it."

"Use the stone to protect yourself," she warns. My father's purple stone, the one that vibrates when I hold it.

"A vampire cannot see themselves in a mirror, and this is true to who they are. They don't know that they are fooling you, and that is part of their curse. Most humans will never see a vampire for who the monster they truly are, because the truth is only revealed right before becoming their victim."

I think of the club, of the girl screaming. Did she see the true monster?

Gramma Sugar nods her head. Mom begins to flicker.

"I trust Conrad," I say.

"Please, Gray, don't trust a vampire. Your father made that mistake once."

And with those words, Mom is gone.

"What do you think?" I ask Gramma Sugar.

"I think I need to rest now." Gramma lies back.

"I'll come back to take you home tomorrow, okay?"

"That sounds nice, dear."

I kiss her on her cheek and leave the room. Hurrying out of the hospital, I continue on my way to see Conrad, so I can decide for myself if all vampires are dangerous.

14

When I arrive at the police station, I text Joe.

Conrad got arrested. I'm at the police station. Call me.

I see three dots. Finally, he is going to talk to me.

They disappear. I try again.

Joe, please. I need to talk to you.

Nothing.

I get out of the car and slam the door shut. The sun sears into my eyes, and I search my bag for my sunglasses. And of course, I drop them. A familiar hand reaches down in front of me and picks them up.

It's Heath.

"Oh, hi, what're you d-doing here?" I stammer, slipping the glasses on.

"I work here," he says, tapping his badge.

"No you don't," I retort. Sure, he's an officer, but not here.

"Well, me and my guy were part of an arrest in an important case, so... But what are you doing here, Gray?" he says, changing topics.

"Important case," I say.

There it is, that tilt of the chin, while his eyes pierce straight into my heart. This time I'm ready — I have armor now. The kind that builds when you lose a mother and a father. This armor is thick, so thick that Heath's allure bounces right off me.

"Why couldn't we make it work?" he asks.

I cough at the unexpected directness.

"You know the answer." Part of me is relieved and the armored part of me feels less protected. It burns. The one thing he and I did have going for us was a deep attraction.

"Why are you asking me this when you're about to get married?"

"Old habits die hard."

"I am not a habit."

He looks at the ground.

"I should probably go." His eyes look hurt. Part of me pities him, because he's about to make a huge mistake, but his own ego is too big for him to see around it.

"How well do you really know Elizabeth?"

"I knew you were jealous."

My sunglasses hide my eyeroll.

"All I'm saying is, make sure you're sure. This is the rest of your life, right?" His hand brushes against mine.

"I'm sure." A pang of some emotion I cannot name moves beneath my armor. He tries to take my hand, and misses. Instead, his hand brushes against mine.

"I hope you get your happily ever after." I head for the station.

"I wish I could be like you, Gray."

I stop and turn.

"How do you mean?"

"You still wish me well, even after the heartbreak."

"Because my heart is just fine," I lie.

15

They have me waiting to see Conrad in a makeshift visitor's room, which is just a tiny, messy office. I peruse the paperwork hanging out of the tray on the desk, and the door opens.

"Gray," Conrad says, and my smile falls. The very short time he's been here at the Salem Street Station has not been kind to him. I almost don't recognize him. His perfect hair fade is uneven, and dark circles rim his eyes. His smooth gait seems disjointed. The officer escorting him handcuffs him to the wooden chair across from me.

"I'll be right outside, just call if you need me," the officer tells me.

I highly doubt this is protocol, allowing a visiting detective to sit alone in a closet-sized office with an accused murderer. However, there is no geometry to allow the three of us to fit into this cramped space. It's also possible that Heath heard I was meeting Conrad and pulled a string or two. The officer closes the door.

"Conrad, are you okay?"

"Just fine," he says and grins. He has lost his luster. He's not giving me goosebumps.

"What do you think they have on you?" I ask.

"Could be anything. Whatever Patrick Bennett wants it to be?"

"The lieutenant governor?"

"Yes. Gray, you know they are framing me. He probably had Izzy do his dirty work."

Something feels off about our conversation. Conrad seems so different, and he's not looking at me.

"Conrad, what do you need me to do?"

"Prove they did it."

"Right, yeah, of course. Is there anything else you can tell me? About that night? About Patrick Bennett?"

"I've told you everything."

I detect the tiniest change in his voice.

"I know, but sometimes we can miss even the most obvious clues."

"There is nothing you don't know."

"Why did Patrick Bennett pick you to frame, then?"

"Convenience. Because I work at the café."

"Or is it because you're a vampire?"

Conrad stares into my eyes, and every pore on my body stands at attention.

"In a lot of ways, we are no different than humans. Vampires can be anybody anywhere."

And I know he is right.

———

As I leave the police station, for the first time I feel like Conrad might not be telling the whole truth. Did I get this wrong? Did he kill Adam Dawson, and I've been some sort of sick toy for him to play with this entire time?

I drop into the driver's seat and check my device.

A text from Joe.

Gray, we should talk.

Well, that's not loaded. Of course, we should talk — I've been trying to talk to you for days now. I want to send him a thirty-page letter of thoughts, but instead I don't respond at all. Put Hero in reverse and go straight to the liquor store.

When I get home, I take account of the facts of my life. My parents are gone. Gramma Sugar's in the hospital. Heath is getting married. Joe hates me. Conrad is a murderer. Okay, so the last two are up for debate, but still.

All of this adds up to me staying up too late, sitting in my cozy chair reading one of my dad's old books with a mug filled with vodka.

I take the shiny purple stone from my pocket and flip it over in my hand. Mom said it would protect me, and she was right. It was in my pocket earlier, when I went to see Conrad.

Could the stone be responsible for his less than shining appearance? Mom had said vampires don't show someone their real selves until just before they are made their victim. And Conrad warned me anyone could be a vampire... Was he being metaphorical? My mind spins with questions. Or maybe it's the alcohol.

I take out my device and start to message Joe.

~~Hey Joe, I could really use a friend~~

No...

~~Joe, wtf do you mean we should talk?? I've been calling/texting!!!~~

Too many exclamation points...

~~Joe—I think I'm falling in lo~~

I delete my final attempt and throw my device across the room and onto the couch. No messages should ever be allowed sent past two a.m. No good can ever come from it.

Better go to bed, so I can pickup Gramma in the morning.

I arrive at the hospital bleary-eyed and caffeinated. Gramma Sugar doesn't make any snarky comments.

"Thank you for taking me home, dear," she says as I shut the car door behind her.

Sitting behind the wheel, when I gaze over at Gramma, she looks smaller. I remember when she held me in her lap as a child, and now I'm the one taking care of her. It feels bittersweet.

She looks at me softly, and says, "Let's get outta here, I don't have all *day*."

"You got it," I say as we leave.

Gramma Sugar fiddles with the music until she gets frustrated and turns it off.

"Gramma, can I ask you something?"

"Why do young people always ask if they can ask? Just get on with the question." She motions with her hands to move forward.

"Do you believe in soulmates?"

She exhales an extra-long breath.

"I believe in soul teachers. Our souls come to this plane to learn, and I look at it like different levels of teachers — you have your kindergarten teacher, who might teach you how to read and then maybe a parent shows you how to think. In surfing school you learn how to administer first aid to a jelly-fish sting. There are teachers who show you heartbreak and grit and communication and loyalty. Most important life lessons are taught by soul teachers." Gramma adjusts her seatbelt.

"I was thinking like a love match." Truthfully, I was thinking about how I didn't think they existed.

"Oh, I know what you meant. Soul teachers are especially skilled in love. Some teach what you want, what you don't want, things that surprise you or things that calm you. And the greatest teacher will turn every lever you have learned upside-down."

"And then what do you do?"

"You study."

"You study being turned upside-down?" This does not sound the least bit romantic.

"Precisely, dear."

"And is there some final exam to study for?"

"Sort of. Your greatest soul teacher will offer you many lessons and then you will learn something more about yourself. You see, Gray, learning about who you are and what is right for you is ever-changing, and the patterns you take from your parents have to be worked out, then the patterns from dealing with that have to be worked out. The soul is like an apple," she says.

"Okay, the soul is an apple, you have my attention." I'm driving slow as to not miss a word.

"You're eating the apple from the skin to the core, and hopefully you get to point where you find the seeds to plant your life the way you'd like it to be. Some people will get there faster than others, some stop at the skin, and some only stare at apple trees longingly and never pick the apple at all."

"Are you getting biblical, Gramma?"

"You hush your mouth," she teases.

"So your great soul teacher is the one that gets you to the core? Did you have one?" I ask.

"Yes, I do," she says.

"Gramma Sugar! Who is it?" I haven't seen a boyfriend lately, and I'm all ears.

We pull into her driveway.

"Well, dear, thank you for the ride. I think I'd like to go and have a nap," she deflects. And I'm stonewalled for the moment. I help her out of the car, knowing that I'll never look at an apple the same way again.

17

THREE DAYS LATER

My nerves feel like they did when we first met for a drink. The Uncanny is now my local bar because Joe converted me. I haven't seen Joe since the night after The Royal Icon.

Pushing through the door, the familiar scent of stale popcorn hits my senses. Joe sits at the bar in his leather jacket; he glances at me like he's been waiting. I'm relieved when his face cracks into an easy grin and there's no sign of the disappointment he wore when he found Conrad and me at my apartment. My heart skips like an old record.

A glass with vodka on ice sits in front of the empty seat next to Joe. Rooster, the bartender, gives me a wink. I sit, unsure of how to greet Joe.

"Thanks for the drink," I say quietly.

"My pleasure," he says in his soft gruff of a voice.

We sit in silent tension; the noises of the bar are blunted by our magnetic force. Finally, I look over to him, and he looks at me. My heart sounds like thunder in my chest, yet neither of us says a word. After a brutally long while, Joe arches an eyebrow.

"You're wearing pants."

I blush. So, we're going to start right in with the fact that the last time I saw him, I was sans pants and only wearing the teeshirt belonging to a vampire who happens to be in jail right now.

"Sorry to disappoint you."

I hope that will cover many bases.

Joe sighs.

"Do you want to tell me about Conrad?" he asks.

"Yes. No. Where've you been? I tried calling and texting."

"Following a lead. I'm sorry, sometimes I get tunnel vision and don't check anything but the time."

"Okay. I think he might have done it," I confess.

"Conrad?"

"Yes."

"Nope."

"How do you know?"

"Cameras."

"Joe, we saw the video from The Crucible's cameras, and we found nothing."

"But I got footage from a camera at the bank across the street from The Crucible. Had to use some favors, and a little bribery, but..."

"I'm sure the police have already seen this," I say.

"The bank was never served a warrant for security footage, a little fact I came across. Without a warrant, the bank had no reason to hand it over." He is smug.

"No reason except to help find a murderer."

"I'm guessing they didn't want to help the police for a reason." He scrolls his phone.

"Strange. Why would a neighbor to a gruesome crime, hold back on evidence?" I wonder.

"Great question. Take a look."

He leans over and shows me the video on his phone.

A color video shows the front of The Crucible, and a man and woman in the bottom frame. They're in black baseball caps and gloves walking toward The Crucible. They're turned away from the camera, so you can't see their faces.

"The thing I can't figure out, is that when they leave the screen they are going directly toward The Crucible, but the only way into the alley is through the café or right by the front door. They never appear on those camera's. There's no back entrance, so it would be impossible for them to get into the alley without appearing on The Crucible's cameras," he says.

"You've narrowed it down enough to know it's a male/female team, but you can't see their faces, so this isn't enough to set Conrad free," I say.

Joe's face lights up.

"Oh, yes you can." He forwards the video.

After sixteen minutes elapse, the two figures come back into frame. Joe pauses the video at a moment when both faces are visible. It's Izzy. And Elizabeth.

"Oh, shoot," I whisper. Heath is marrying a killer. The police officer is marrying a criminal. He won't believe it, unless there is definitive proof.

"You know them?" Joe asks.

"Yes, but not really *know*. Met them. Once." I stumble on my words.

Joe looks surprised.

"Okay, my turn to fill you in. The guy is Izzy, Patrick Bennett's new assistant, and the girl is Elizabeth. She's marrying my... The night I went to The Royal Icon, things got messy," I say.

Joe's paying attention.

"Izzy revealed he saw Adam Dawson. He gave me some details about the murder he shouldn't have known, and now we know why. Conrad went off somewhere with this girl, Asha, but first he saved me from Izzy and a crew of vampires. Then Izzy and I got into it while I was waiting to leave. He covered my mouth. I lost consciousness." I quickly side-eye Joe to see if he's with me. He is. His grip tightens on his beer.

"Conrad took me home, and then you saw me the next morning," I finished.

"What happened between getting saved and me showing up at your place? Wait. Stop. Don't tell me," he says.

It's strange seeing Joe so indecisive.

"Joe, nothing happened," I say, trying to assuage any jealousy.

"You know, I'm not oblivious to what I saw. It's okay, you are free to live your life. I just hope ... you'll be careful when it comes to..."

"Vampires. Yes, I know, super dangerous," I say, realizing he's not jealous. Maybe I wanted him to be a little jealous.

"You're right, I'll try and be more cautious about my night-time investigating habits," I state, my voice rising.

"That sounded terrible."

I laugh at the unintended comedy of my word choice.

Before long we are both leaning over in hysterics.

"Okay, okay," I say, trying to stabilize.

"Not okay." He's still wheezing. I lean in close to him.

"Joe, I know how they got into the alley."

He comes even closer.

"How?"

"They levitated."

His eyes become as big as full moons. And we are laughing again.

And when I look at him, the world moves in slow motion. I run our first meeting through my mind — he was so confident, which made me furious. The way he understood me and even liked me when I was being myself. It felt supernatural. Not the meeting; I meet new people all the time, it's my job. The energy between us flared like a meteor shower.

It does every time we're together.

I'm sensitive to all these feelings.

I always choose this. In people, in experiences ... in a job.

Choosing a job that includes intense emotional stimulation is either a genius plan of exposure therapy for sensitivity or plain sadomasochism.

Joe feels like neither. He is a mystery, because he is both intense and a comfort.

I'm a detective, and I'm good at it.

Maybe he's my most challenging case yet.

18

How do I prove that Heath's fiancée Elizabeth and Izzy killed Adam Dawson? The video does put them at the crime scene at the correct time, but without evidence they were in the alley it's a no-go.

Levitation would be an impossible sell to the police.

It does surprise me Heath would make such a tragic mistake in choosing his future wife. I'd be lying if I didn't feel insulted that we'd be in the same dating pool. I'm sure she has many decent qualities, but when they have their deep talks, aren't there clues that indicate potential homicidal tendencies?

Seeing the video shocked me. I was starting to let the drama go, let my mind be free, let him marry someone living the vampire nightlife. He might already know about it and approve, be cool with it. It's their business. But then she shows up on that video.

And I know that he can't know this. Participating in or being witness to a murder, that I am sure goes against Heath's very nature. He wants to protect people, and he wants to be the hero. An echo of pain hits my stomach for the way this is going to shake him.

I take another sip of my latte and scroll through my case file. The social media photo of Adam Dawson from his social media at the beach stares back at me. I look at the totem on his neck. *Who gave it to him?*

I call Joe.

"Joe, I have to go back to The Royal Icon."

"I'm sorry, did I hear you correctly?" he asks.

"I know. But I need to find out something that only a vampire can tell me."

"Why don't you ask Conrad?"

"Because if he could answer my question, I doubt he would have hired me in the first place."

"Well, then I'm going with you."

"Okay."

"Okay? When?"

"Yes, okay. Tonight."

19

This time I drive us to The Royal Icon and I skip the mini-dress, opting for black leather pants and suede flat boots. Now I won't be inhibited by my outfit. Joe is also in all black, except for his famous leather jacket. We are undercover, both wearing our fake totems, which I secured for five Coin each in a gift shop on the main drag in Salem.

We enter the same way I did with Conrad; the door opens on its own when we approach it. The lights inside are red, and it makes everyone in the club appear to have blood-red skin as they dance to the supremely loud beat. We make our way into the crowd, and I lead Joe to the table by the VIP suite, where Conrad and I had sat. I figure we can set up shop and look for someone I recognize from my first visit.

We sit, and Joe is wide-eyed looking around.

"This is something," he says.

"I thought you'd been here before."

"Only during the day, when it was closed. And that was just to talk about the insurance."

"Oh. Yes, it's a little overstimulating."

"Now what is the plan?" he asks.

"Waiting to see someone I recognize."

I look around at everyone and remember my discovery from last time. I tap Joe, and point up, so he can see the levitating vampires. He looks at them in wonder and then back at me and we laugh. *What is this life we are leading?*

My phone vibrates. I check it.

It's Lucy.

Sorry, Lucy, but it's bad timing. Again. I decline her call.

When will it be a good time to call her? Certainly not when I'm at a vampire club searching for a lead on a killer.

Scanning the crowd, seeking anyone familiar, I think I see the face of the girl in blue sequins from the VIP suite. But then she disappears back into the crowd like a wave that crests then dips back into the ocean.

Joe notices my focus. "See someone?"

"I thought I did, but she kind of faded into the crowd. I think I'm going to cross the room and see if it's her?"

"Should I come with or hang here?"

"You stay; this will be our meeting spot."

"Got it, I'll be right here."

There is this easy strength in Joe, and it's soothing. I trust he will be right there.

"This shouldn't take long," I say, and I depart for the dance floor.

Everyone is squeezed together, so it's hard to make my way through the labyrinth while also checking faces. But then I spot her. Tonight, she wears a blue fringe dress. It's the girl who was sitting with Izzy. The one who took some of my candy-not-really-drugs-drugs.

I try to angle under someone's arm to move closer, but when I come up, she's gone again. It's a game of Twister with hungry vampires.

Their charms are blocked by the shiny purple stone zipped

into my pocket. I spot the woman again, and head toward her, but as I move forward, someone spins me around.

And I'm face-to-face with Asha. Conrad's ex-or-current girlfriend.

"Asha," I can't help but confirm aloud.

"What are you doing here?" She looks disgusted.

"Can we talk?" I ask. I came here to speak with a vampire, and if it's not the sequins girl, then Asha will do.

"Uh, no," she says and turns to go in a dramatic fashion.

"It could help free Conrad," I rush to say.

This stops her.

Slowly, she turns back to face me.

"Let's go to a table." I signal for her to follow me, as there is no chance of carrying on a conversation out here. When we arrive at the table where I left Joe, I'm flustered that he is not there. Where he promised to stay. But I can't lose this potential lead, so I hope he is doing something safe and worthwhile.

"I need to know something about Adam Dawson," I say, cutting straight to it.

"Yes," she says.

"Yes, you know him?"

"Yes."

"Adam was wearing this when he died." I hold up my phone and show her the photo of Adam wearing the totem.

"So?"

"Do you know who gave it to him?" I ask, but what I really want to say is. "Which one of you bloodsucker's did he *belong* to?"

"Of course. Patrick Bennett."

"Patrick Bennett? Lieutenant Governor Patrick Bennett? Married with children Patrick Bennett?"

"Yes."

I feel like I could ask Asha anything and she would merely answer yes. I scan the vicinity for Joe. Where did he go?

"So, why would Patrick's new assistant murder Adam?"

She doesn't even blink at my assumption.

"Mr. Bennett is a very possessive man."

"Adam was seeing someone else."

Her body language says I'm right, although it looks like the tiniest semblance of a tear is forming in her eyes. Now it dawns on me.

"Conrad," I say delicately.

She wipes the tear away before it hits her cheek.

"And that's why Bennett framed him."

Asha looks at the floor.

"I'm sorry, Asha." Her pain is palpable. She gets up and disappears into the crowd.

Joe returns, and I freeze when I see he's holding drinks. Conrad's warning about not drinking anything at the club echoes in my brain.

"You didn't drink anything, did you?"

I swat the drinks out of his hands; the glasses smash onto the floor and the contents spray onto both of us.

"Just a sip," he says.

Oh no. What is going to happen to Joe?

I grab his hand and pull him back through the crowd to the exit.

"Ah can't fewah my mow ... " He's tongue-tied.

He stumbles as I get him out the door, and I prop him up against the building while I call for an AutoVehicle. I'll have to come back for Hero later. Two minutes pass and we get inside the car. In seconds, Joe is asleep on my shoulder.

I hope sleep is all that happens.

20

Exhaustion meets the sunrise. I've been up most of the night, making sure Joe is still breathing. He was fitful on my couch, and sometimes it looked like he was too still, and I'd freeze and watch and make sure his chest still rose and fell.

Just after dawn, he starts to wake.

"Gray? Am I at your place?"

"Yes, but don't worry, you're still wearing all your own clothes."

He doesn't have the energy to laugh, but his eyes shine.

"Let me get you some coffee." I bring it to him as he sits up. It looks like he might be in pain.

"What happened?"

"I may have forgotten to warn you about drinking anything at The Royal Icon. It was one of Conrad's rules."

"What rule?

"To not."

"To not what?"

"To not drink anything, not even water."

"How could you forget that?"

"I'm sorry, I didn't even think of it. I was just so focused on getting the intel. And you were supposed to stay at the table anyway."

"Did you get information?"

"I did. Adam Dawson belonged to Patrick Bennett, but then he had a side thing with Conrad. Apparently, that didn't go over so well with Bennett. Hence, murder and mayhem."

"How did you find all of this out?"

"Asha, Conrad's girlfriend."

"Jeez — the love lives of vampires. Tragic."

"Shakespearian."

"We still need to prove that Elizabeth and Izzy were in that alley."

"Cookies for breakfast?" I ask.

"You lead the way," Joe says.

———

When we get to The Crucible, it still doesn't open for another five minutes.

"I guess we wait," Joe says.

"Or..." I say, scanning the area.

"Let's recreate their steps, Elizabeth and Izzy." I offer. Joe brings up the video and we watch it again.

"Okay, that is from the camera there," I say. We mark the spot where they enter the frame with a rock. I pull Joe forward toward the street, and he takes photos as we go.

"They walked this way," I mutter. "And this is where they disappear from the frame." I stop in the middle of the street. Luckily no cars are on the road this early.

"But now what did they do after that?"

"Well, if you were going to hide out of sight to levitate into the alley where would you go?"

"There." I point to a nearby tree someone could easily hide behind.

As Joe and I walk over to the tree, I see a glint of light in The Crucible's window. It's the reflection of Joe's jacket zipper.

"Wait, walk by the window again," I say.

I hurry over to The Crucible's camera and record my own video from it's angle.

"We need to look at The Crucible's video again," I say.

"Gray, we've already watched it a million times. And the police have too, and the lawyers. Don't think you'll find anything."

"So, what's one more time?" I smile.

Just then the door pushes open, and an employee puts out the cauldron with specials onto the sidewalk.

"Perfect timing."

Inside, we sit at a table and watch the video from the day of Adam Dawson's murder. This time we see what we had all missed before. This time we see the reflection of Elizabeth's one-of-a-kind, serpent-shaped totem in the window.

"It's enough to have her questioned."

I scream silently and kick my feet. Joe fake screams too. I live for this feeling. It's beyond exhilaration.

21

The message *LOADING COMPLETE* blinks on the screen of my device.

The thumb drive is loaded with all my files on Conrad's case, the photos and video and my typed-out report of what I think happened. I remove the thumb drive and add it to a manila envelope. There is no way for me to do what has to happen next without destroying Heath in the process, so I've decided to send everything to the police anonymously.

I make a call to Conrad.

"Conrad, I think I may have figured out how to get you your freedom."

"Oh, wow. Thank you, Gray," he says.

"I know about Adam. Why didn't you tell me?"

He's quiet for moment.

"There is no way you would have believed me that I didn't do it." He's right.

"I'm sorry."

"Me too."

"Take care, Conrad. I'll be in touch."

As we hang up, I receive a message. It's Heath.

Gray, are you coming to the wedding? Need a final count for the caterer.

Crap. How is there still a wedding? I look over at the envelope, the one that will destroy everything for him.

I text Joe.

Hey, Joe. You want to come to a wedding with me on Saturday?

Joe begins responding right away. I can only imagine what he's thinking. After he disappeared for three days last week after finding me with Conrad, I'm relieved he's back to his old reliable self. A minute later, he sends a message back.

Yes.

And now I must respond to Heath.

~~Heath, you can't marry her, she's a mur~~
~~Why do you want me to be there?~~
~~I'm bringing Joe, he's the most amazing man. You'll abso-~~
~~lutely hate~~

I take a deep breath, type and hit send.

Yes. Plus one.

22

I t's afternoon and I'm undecided. It's a complicated thing selecting what to wear to watch your ex-fiancé marry a murderous vampire lover. Torn between a long, black dress, fitted and flattering that says, *this is your funeral, buddy* or the short, red dress that says, *your loss, asshole*. All while simultaneously considering my date — Joe. I snatch the red one off the hanger and pull it on. With my trusty trench coat, I feel ready.

Joe shows up tieless in a crisp, white button-down and predictably his leather jacket. He's eating an apple.

"You're wearing that?" I ask.

He points to my trench.

"Are you wearing that?"

We counter-smile with our eyes.

"Gray, you take my damn breath."

"That's a good thing?" I'm flirting now.

"So good." He finishes the apple, and I think about what Gramma said.

"Well, you clean up finely yourself there, partner."

"We going to make it on time?"

"Yes — I should fill you in on a few things on the way," I prepare.

We go out to my car, Hero.

Once in the car and facing the road, I feel less tense about telling Joe.

"So, this wedding is for Heath and Elizabeth."

"Elizabeth Wagner. From the video?"

"Yes."

"She's not in custody yet?"

"Apparently not, but...Heath is —"

"One poor dude."

"Yes, and he's my ex."

Joe's face clenches.

"Whoa," is all he says.

"I know. Ex-fiancé, actually."

"Wait. You were going to marry the same guy as this criminal lady is about to marry?"

"It gets worse," I tell him, and now I realize this may be the worst date in the history of all dates.

"Okay." He looks steady. And now I'm about to make him unsteady.

"He's a cop. Massachusetts State Patrol."

"He's a Statie? Oh, shit."

"I know."

"And I thought you invited me because you liked me, but this is definitely a work call, isn't it?" His words sound more hurt than he looks.

"I do like you. And yes, it's sort of a personal-meets-work-meets-personal sort of thing."

"Damn, Gray."

"You seem pleased."

"Excited. We always seem to get into trouble together and if the trouble solves cases, then it's a double bonus."

I laugh nervously. Because even if Joe is onboard, we are still going to Heath's wedding. The police should definitely have opened my evidence package by now. Anything could happen.

23

When we arrive at the venue, a huge white tent is staged with a view of the ocean. Waves of men in navy uniforms mingle amongst the guests. A girl in a floral dress offers us a small pink bottle of bubbles as we enter.

"For the aisle walk," she says, then rushes away toward the couple behind us.

I stare at the cushioned white chairs set up for the ceremony.

"Bride's side or groom's side?" someone asks.

We meet each other face to face. It's Gwen, Heath's mother.

"Gray? Is that you?" she asks. This woman is the epitome of the town gossip. She knows what everyone is doing at all times — with whom and when and why. Little does she know, her own family is about to be central in some epic gossip.

I've come to think of gossip as a defense mechanism. Why not meddle in the affairs of others, rather than tend to your own? It offers Gwen an escape from dealing with her own life, and because of this I feel great compassion toward her. However, at this moment I would like to escape from her as quickly as possible.

"Wonderful to see you again, Mrs. Tyler," I say.

Just then, a harried woman in a bridesmaid's gown runs up and grabs onto Gwen's forearm.

"Um, I was told to get you right away. Heathy needs you."

"Oh." And without a glance back at me she is gone. I look to the sky and mouth *Thank you*.

"Dodged a bullet there, eh?" Joe says.

"Ha!" I say too loud. I grab his hand and lead him to some seats near the back. I try and avoid eye contact with any guest I might know or not know. Suddenly my skin crawls from the thought of having to engage with people I knew eons ago, when I was a different person.

Joe and I huddle together as the string quartet begins playing Schubert. Heath, looking fit and slightly nervous as his hand plays with a button on the chest of his uniform, makes his way down the aisle.

And this is probably the first time I allow myself to let in the heartsick feeling of Heath getting married. To someone who's not me. I thought I resolved this a long time ago, but watching him stand up there has me questioning said resolution. He is not, was not the right person for me, but even still he looks so ... happy. The musicians stop and stand, and we see her. And him. I'm aghast.

Elizabeth stands at the back of the aisle, on the arm of Lieutenant Governor Patrick Bennett. Her auburn curls are half tied back into a tiara, her constellation of freckles now covered by foundation and perfect pink blush. The flowing organza gown is completely outshone by the serpent totem dangling from a chain around her neck.

"Is that —" Joe whispers.

"Patrick Bennett," I confirm.

All of the discontent about the case and the wedding stir together inside my stomach, and I feel sick. Just as she reaches Heath, I understand this is really happening. I am a witness.

Heath is marrying a murderer.

As Heath stares into Elizabeth's evil eyes to speak his vows, Joe taps me lightly on the arm. I didn't realize I was clutching the tiny bottle of bubbles so hard the liquid was leaking through my fingers. I drop it into the grass and Joe hands me a tissue from his jacket. I'm not sure if I should wipe my hand or my eyes.

Just then movement at the back of the tent catches my attention. Several uniformed officers make their way down the aisle. Heath smiles, like he is about to be surprise-serenaded by his coworkers performing in some elaborate musical number. But we all watch as his eyes turn to panic. I clutch Joe, much like I did the poor bubble container.

Two men take Heath aside and tell him something. He's livid, barking back at them. All the while two others cuff Elizabeth, reading her Miranda rights. One of the arresting officers steps on her organza gown and she trips. Humiliations pile up, as she cries and her perfect mascara begins to run. She briefly clocks me with her gaze, as she passes our row. Is it malice or defiance I see?

I can't bear looking at Heath.

Joe gently takes my hand and guides us out of the frenzied crowd, which sounds loud, shocked and angry.

itting at my desk at Strange Investigations, while Joe sits thoughtfully on the arm of the chair. We are sitting in the same positions as when we first met Conrad. Our office is still new, but the ache of this case sits heavy on the both of us. We're still wearing our wedding garb, although my heels found their place in the corner by the door immediately upon our entry.

I'm eating the remains of the Mongolian beef we ordered for dinner and Joe is finishing off his chow mein.

My phone buzzes. Joe stops chewing and looks over.

"Gray Cooper," I answer.

"Hi Gray, it's Conrad." I mouth *Con-rad* to Joe.

"Are you okay?" I ask.

"More than okay — I'm out," he says, sheer joy in his voice.

"Ohmygod, Conrad, great, that's amazing, insane news." I can't think of any more hyperbole right now.

"You did it. I knew you would," he said. I can hear music and chatter in the background.

"I'm so happy for you, Conrad, truly."

"I'll be back at The Crucible in the morning if you want to come by," he says.

"I'll one hundred percent be there."

"Conrad, let's go." It's Asha I hear in the background.

"I've got to go, thanks again," he says.

"Have a fun night, you deserve it," I hang up.

Then I stand up from my desk, take off my coat and swing it over my head like I'm at a sports event.

Because, I, Detective Gray Cooper, just helped my client return to freedom. Joe likely thinks I've lost my sensibility, but if he thought I had any to begin with, that was a bad decision on his part.

"Good news?"

"Conrad is out and *we* helped him," I sing.

"Great news."

"Congratulations, partner." I hold up my can of Coke Zero, and he cheers-taps it with his bottle of water.

"Cheers to Strange Investigations," I say.

As if my emotional bandwidth for the day wasn't already at full tilt. Joe leans in, like this is going to be it. The moment's thick with hope and excitement, and I inhale the air between us. I lean in for a kiss, but his arms fold around me, so I pull back. Instead of the kiss I expected, we embrace. I feel disappointed and relieved. We just hold each other a long while.

"Joe?"

"Gray?"

"Thank you for being there with me today. It was a lot for me on many levels," I say head on his chest.

"On the rings of Saturn?" he asks.

I remember the conversation when I asked him to partner with me on Strange Investigations. I'd joked we might find ourselves on the rings of Saturn.

"It's the only place I expect to go," I respond.
And then there isn't anything more to say.

26

My alarm blazes early, and I stumble through my morning routine and get myself out the door so that I can get to the coffee shop.

It's hard not to think of Elizabeth and Izzy as I cross the same street I recorded footage with Joe on so we could report them.

Once inside The Crucible, I spot Conrad behind the counter. He looks at me with those amber eyes and I remember I'm without my purple stone protector. Goose-bumps climb my arms.

"I'm happy to see you here," I tell him.

"Me too," he says.

"Good morning." I hear a familiar, cheerful voice behind me.

I turn to find Lucy, my smart friend with a lion's mane of caramel curls.

"Lucy." My heart softens, yet fear edges my voice. What is she doing here? Are we still friends? She hugs me hard.

Hugging your best friend after a long time apart is a homecoming. We release the hug and she sees the apology on my face.

"I'm so sorry," I say.

"I understand and accept. You don't always make it easy for the people who love you to love you," she says.

"You're right. And there's so much I have to tell you and —" I reach out to hug her again.

"Let's get some coffee," she exclaims.

We order and find a table.

"Luce, how have you been?"

"Well, I'm still getting my hours working under Dr. Hamilton. Only one hundred left."

"That's incredible. You are so close. You're going to make a great therapist."

"What's been going on with you? Are you seeing someone to deal with your grief?"

My stomach aches. "I'm not."

"I'll give you a card for someone." She digs in her gigantic leather purse.

"Okay, but, Luce, um, a lot has happened. I honestly don't know where to start..."

"Gramma Sugar?"

"She's good. Had to get a pacemaker but on the mend and her same old spicy self."

"I love her. Okay, dating anyone?"

"You know I've sworn off dating."

"Ugh, right, because of dreamboat-asshole Heath."

"So, Heath ... almost got married on Saturday."

"Whhhhaaaatt. You're kidding. To who?"

"I went to the wedding. She got arrested before it started and we left."

"Hold up, hold up. Arrested? And...*we? We* who?"

"Joe and I."

I take a deep breath and fill her in on Joe and Strange Investigations. I tell her about my first case, the Vondales and the aliens. It's an easier story than the one I was about to tell her about Mom.

"Gray, your life is like an opera these days. You can never ghost me again."

That is an apropos choice of words. My heart beats faster, at the thought of telling her the rest.

"I know, you're right. There's another thing — and this one is way out there."

"Farther than a detective case about aliens?"

"Well, actually I didn't tell you about the vampires." I see Conrad look over from the pastry case and smile.

"Lucy, my mom is a ghost."

"Oh, honey."

"Like she visits me."

"Okay, let me give you Dr. Simmons card, she'll help you work through this. She's a genius." She starts fishing through her purse again.

She doesn't believe me, but she loves me.

"You're like a therapy rolodex."

"I am, aren't I?" She jams another card at me. "Okay, I hate to leave this wild convo, but I have a session at ten."

"I'm so happy to see you and to catch up."

"Me too, Coops."

"Let's do this again, maybe next week?"

"Yes." She gets up. "Call Dr. Simmons."

"I'll think about it."

"Dooo it," she says as she hugs me goodbye.

27

TWO DAYS LATER

My bare feet are cold on the wood floor in the morning as the tea kettle blows. I turn the burner off and pour hot water into two teacups. One for me and one for Gramma. She's propped in an armchair with cushions and an afghan.

"Your tea, my lady," I offer.

"Thanks, dear."

"Do you want to watch a film or play poker?"

"Neither."

"Whoa. Gramma, what will we ever do today if you refuse your favorite pastimes twice in a row?"

"Have you seen your mother lately?"

"Not since the last time I was here."

"Hmmm."

"Am I supposed to?"

"Well, I've been wondering if she'd return since you had this vampire case."

"Gramma, I told you the case is closed." I did not, however, tell her that Heath's fiancée was the prime suspect. Her case is awaiting trial. Izzy has disappeared and Heath hasn't returned any of my messages. Can't blame him. A guy with an ego his size is unlikely to recover from a humiliation so large very quickly.

"What happened with Dad?" I ask.

"The vampire and Dad?" She takes a large gulp of tea. "There was a case, a woman called Lenora. The second your father took the case, Madeline was unhappy. She thought this Lenora held Woody under some sort of spell."

I thought of my own experience with Conrad and his mesmerizing aura.

"Can vampires do that?"

"Yes, in fact, it's the main thing they do."

"What happened with Lenora?" I ask, not sure if I really want to hear this.

"Despite your mother's protests, Woody was determined to solve the case."

This is uncomfortably relatable.

"What was the case?"

"Missing person. Lenora told Woody it was her brother Odell. Woody found him. Turns out it wasn't her brother at all."

"Oh, no."

"Turns out the man was actually hiding from Lenora. She'd given him some necklace."

A totem.

"So, Dad turned this guy over to her?" I asked nervously.

"Yes, because that's what she paid him to do. And this Odell, he disappeared for real afterward. Your mother was able to break Lenora's spell over Woody, by slipping a crystal into his pocket for protection."

"Woody was overcome with grief, when he realized the truth he'd been deceived. He wouldn't stop searching for

Odell, feeling like he served him up on a platter to Lenora. He wanted to make it right."

"That's awful."

"When you work in the paranormal, Gray, you'll find just as much darkness in the supernatural world as you will in the mainstream one." A chill moves up my neck.

Doubts fill my heart.

"Then why should I do it? Why work in this field at all?"

"Because my dear, there will always be bad actors and horrible truths, but you are a curator of the light. Pursuing what's good and right. And even a small act of goodness has repercussions much deeper and widespread than evil ever could. Don't ever let the darkness keep you from finding the light."

Gramma Sugar reaches over and holds my hand, her grip stronger than her eighty years should allow for.

And I know that she's right.

"Gramma, you never told me who your greatest soul teacher is," I say quietly.

Her eyes soften.

"It's you, my dear."

The sky is clear and blue as I drive to the office on this brisk morning. Pulling into the parking lot for the plaza that includes Joe's business Mistwell Insurance and our company Strange Investigations.

I walked by Mistwell, but the sign still says they're closed. Joe must've slept in. There is a certain kick in my step after solving case number two. I'm considering giving Dr. Simmons a call, not that I think it will help me understand my relationship with my ghost mother, but I am aware that I've been under a lot of stress lately. Maybe the therapist could offer me some self-care tools that don't include vodka?

As I approach the office, I notice someone is standing by the door.

Waiting for me.

A woman faces away from me. She turns around and I see that I know her.

"Deborah?"

"Gray," she says, sounding half-panicked. It's Lucy's mom.

"Gray, have you seen Lucy?"

"Yes, just three days ago." I smile.

"No one has heard from her since."

"What?"

"Dr. Hamilton called me. Lucy hasn't been to the office, and her apartment is empty. I'm terrified. She left her purse and her phone. Her door was unlocked. Gray, you've got to help me find her."

My heart drops right out of my body.

Deborah is shaking. I grip her shoulders, like I'm steadying the Earth's rotation.

"We will find her. I promise you."

AFTERWORD

If you enjoyed this book and want to be updated on the next in the series and learn more about my other work.

Please follow my instagram: @jenniferleelauer

Join my free newsletter The Delicate Papers with the QR below
      (there is a paid option for more writerly treats):

Jennifer Lauer is the author of THE GIRL IN THE ZOO and THE STRANGE CHRONICLES series.

A #1 Amazon International Bestseller, her work blends emotional depth with speculative and paranormal themes. The BookLife Prize praised her debut as "especially original, riveting, and timely," while Kirkus Reviews noted its "soft center under the hardware."

 instagram.com/jenniferleelauer
 tiktok.com/@jenniferscifi

Start Somewhere: The Strange Chronicles (2024)

THE GIRL IN THE ZOO (2023)